by Judy Baer

illustrated by Janetta Lewis

Published by Willowisp Press, Inc.
10100 SBF Drive, Pinellas Park, Florida 34666

Printed in the United States of America

10 9 8 7 6 5 4 3 2 1

ISBN 0-87406-469-4

To
Shawnaly, Laura, Jessica, Margaret, Moses,
John, Lisa, Danny, Michael, and Tony

One

PACKING a suitcase is the pits. Packing for a month at camp is even worse. I glanced at the letter from Camp Pinetree that listed the kind of clothes I should bring and tucked one more sweatshirt into the suitcase. I hoped it didn't rain the whole time I was there.

"Becky, are you packed?" my mom called.

"Almost," I answered. "I just have to pack my bubble gum and my posters."

"Good," she replied. "And please don't bring any of that horrible gum home with you at the end of the month!"

I grinned as I slipped packs of Triple Tropical Bubble Gum into my suitcase. It fit nicely into all the little cracks and spaces not filled up by my clothes.

Bubble gum is my trademark. Triple Tropical is my brand. It tastes like bananas, strawberries, and pineapples. I never go anywhere without it.

My mom is a little touchy about my chewing bubble gum. I suppose that's because I have a bad habit of leaving it in places it isn't supposed to be. Every time she finds a wad of Triple Tropical stuck under a piece of furniture or clogging up her dishwasher, she freaks. Mothers can be so touchy sometimes.

I stared out the window and tried to imagine what Camp Pinetree would be like. My dad said there were a lot of pretty trees there. Dad had gone to Camp Evergreen, across the lake from Camp Pinetree, when he was a boy. And he said that even in July it gets chilly at night because of the lake. Dad said there were lots of bugs, too.

I'm not crazy about crawly things, but I

figure I can live with that. What's strange is going to a brand new place where I don't know anyone. I've never had to make new friends before. I've gone to Justice Elementary School for almost my whole life.

Just then the telephone rang, interrupting my thoughts. I picked up the receiver. It was my friend, Lissa. "When do you leave for camp?" she asked.

"As soon as my dad gets home from the office. I hope he takes his time."

"Are you scared?" Lissa asked. "About going to camp, I mean."

"A little," I admitted. "I wish I was more interesting."

"What do you mean?" Lissa asked. "You seem okay to me."

This was hard to explain to Lissa, who thought I was plenty interesting already. I think she's just used to me. We've been friends forever.

"It's my big chance to make a good impression," I said to Lissa. "This is the first time I've ever been with people who haven't known me all my life."

"So what?" Lissa asked, not getting the point at all. "By the end of the month, you'll all be friends anyway."

Lissa didn't understand. She's a very happy person. She's satisfied with the way her life is going. But me, I'm always looking for something better.

For one thing, it's always been my dream to be popular. *Really* popular. At Justice Elementary School there are only a few really popular girls and I'm not one of them. I don't have long, blond hair or blue eyes, and boys sure don't crowd around me.

The thing is, I'm too ordinary to be popular. There's nothing outstanding about me. My hair is pale brown. Even though it's thick and shiny, it's nothing special. My eyes are the same color as my hair. Sometimes people say I'm pretty—if they notice me, that is.

My dad is a dentist and my mother is a housewife. Talk about dull. Even my older sister, Barbara, is ordinary. She goes to college and wants to become a teacher. Boring!

The most interesting thing about me is that I play the guitar. I've taken lessons for six months and I'm getting better all the time.

While Lissa talked, I made faces into a mirror. No matter how hard I tried, I couldn't make my pink cheeks and short nose look interesting. I looked exactly like the 10-year-old girl I am.

"Becky, are you listening to me?" Lissa asked. "You aren't saying much."

I made one last face in the mirror. "Sorry, I was just thinking how dull my life is."

"Dull? You're leaving for camp this afternoon! You'll have all kinds of adventures!"

We talked for a few more minutes, but then Lissa's mother called her. "I have to go now," Lissa said. "Have fun. Write!"

As I hung up the phone, I thought about

our conversation some more. Maybe my life *was* dull right now—and maybe I wasn't very interesting right now—but that could change. This afternoon I'd be going to Camp Pinetree. I didn't have to be ordinary there. I could be popular!

I started to get excited about the idea. This was my big chance to start over, to make new friends. Why hadn't I thought of it before? No one at Camp Pinetree knew Becky Blair. The Becky who arrived at camp didn't have to be the same boring girl Lissa knew. I could be someone interesting—someone special!

Suddenly, I was very eager to finish my packing. I sang a song as I tucked more bubble gum into my suitcase.

"Are you ready? Here I come.
Struttin' my stuff, lookin' real tough,
This is my chance to show the world who I am.
Are you ready? Here I come!"
The words were from a song by Eric

Richards and Outta Site, my favorite singer and rock band in the entire world.

Outta Site is the greatest band ever, but it wouldn't be nearly as good if Eric Richards weren't the lead singer. He's only seventeen years old, but already very famous. I'd heard rumors that Eric grew up in a town not too far from my own house. That made us practically neighbors or something!

I wrote Eric two fan letters last month. I hoped there'd be an answer from him when I came home from camp. I'd told him how much I like his band and how I have his posters all over my room. I even sent him a few sticks of Triple Tropical for an extra treat.

I checked each item in my suitcase against the list Camp Pinetree had sent. When I was sure I had everything I was supposed to have, I pulled two large posters of Eric and Outta Site from the wall and gently put them on top of my clothes.

I looked down and saw my dog, Ruffles,

sitting by my feet. It was hard to go to camp for a month and leave him behind. But it was *impossible* to leave Eric behind!

Besides, if I was going to impress the people at Camp Pinetree and become popular, *really* popular, having the posters couldn't hurt. Maybe just looking at Eric's friendly, familiar face would help me to be more exciting. Or at least not dull.

"Ready, Becky?" my dad called from the bottom of the stairs as he came in the front door. "We've got a long drive to Camp Pine-tree."

There was no turning back now. I was on my way.

*   *   *   *   *

The trees near Camp Pinetree were taller than any I'd ever seen before. I felt as though we were driving through a dark green tunnel carved through the woods. The trees were so tall they looked like they were touching the sky.

"Yes, indeed, Becky, the best memories of my childhood came from going to camp," Dad said as he turned down a narrow, winding dirt road. He gently braked and turned left at a wooden sign announcing we had arrived at Camp Pinetree. "Here we are!" Dad said. "What a great place!"

In the middle of the tall trees was a big, round clearing where a flagpole stood. A red, green, and yellow flag with the words CAMP PINETREE on it flew from the top of the pole.

There were log cabins in a circle facing the clearing. The largest building had a big sign saying FOOD HALL over the door. The little building next to it had a small sign that said PINE CONE STORE. A tiny stream looped between the two buildings, which were connected by a little wooden bridge. Through the trees, I could see a clear blue lake in the distance. I could hear water bubbling in the stream and the wind moving in the treetops.

Everything about Camp Pinetree was beautiful, at least what I could see through the car window. It was as if we'd driven into a brand new world.

"There's the administration building and the nurse's quarters," Dad pointed out. "If you ever need to call home or aren't feeling well, that's where you go."

At that moment, a girl about the age of my older sister came to the car door. She was wearing shorts and a T-shirt with CAMP PINETREE written on the front.

"Welcome to Camp Pinetree!" she said with a smile as wide as a slice of watermelon. She checked notes on the clipboard she was carrying. "You must be Becky Blair."

"How did you know that?" I asked.

"You're one of the last to arrive. My name is Lani Murphy and I'm your counselor."

Lani had short, dark hair that fell in little curls around her face. Her eyes were deep, dark blue and they sparkled with happiness. I liked her right away.

"You're in cabin eight, Becky." Lani pointed down the road. "It's the last cabin on the right. There's a tree stump out front with a big eight painted on it. It's a great cabin to be in. Lots of old timers."

"Old timers?" I echoed and made a face. I was only ten. What did I want to do with a bunch of old campers?

Lani laughed. "They aren't old people, Becky! That just means the girls were at Camp Pinetree last year. They can help you find your way around camp very quickly."

"Oh," I blushed. I wasn't going to impress anyone that way. Maybe it was a good thing I'd be meeting a few old timers.

Dad slid the car into gear and moved slowly around the driveway to the front of cabin eight. It was a cozy log cabin with big, net-covered windows. A squirrel was eating sunflower seeds on the front step and curious faces were peering out the windows.

"Well, Becky," Dad said, "let's get your things unloaded and settled into the cabin. I see your cabin mates are waiting for you."

The girls filed out one by one to watch us.

Suddenly, I thought of the words to the song I'd been singing as I packed my suitcase. This was *my* chance to show the world who I was. And I was going to do it.

Look out Camp Pinetree!

Two

MY stomach fluttered with nervousness as I watched my dad drive away. Luckily, Lani wouldn't let me be nervous for long.

"I want you to meet your new cabin mates, Becky. You're the only girl in cabin eight who wasn't at Camp Pinetree last year. The other girls are old friends now. They'll have lots to tell you. You'll feel right at home in no time."

Somehow I doubted that. It would be hard to make friends in a group of girls who already knew each other.

"Becky, this is Denni Ferguson," Lani bubbled.

Denni was tall and had blond hair and huge blue eyes. She stepped forward and looked me

over from head to toe.

"Denni's grandfather donated the land for this camp. Her parents still own a cabin on the other side of the lake," Lani told me.

"I've been to Camp Pinetree three years in a row," Denni boasted.

My heart sank. There was no way I was going to impress Denni Ferguson with anything I might have to say!

"This is Meg Whitefeather," Lani said, pointing to a girl with golden brown skin. She had high cheekbones and beautiful black hair and eyes.

"This is my second year at Camp Pinetree," Meg said. "I like to dance and draw and..." she added, wrinkling her nose, "I think sugar is very bad for you. I hope you don't eat a lot of candy."

I gulped, thinking of all the Triple Tropical Bubble Gum in my suitcase. It was just my luck to get a health nut for a cabin mate!

Before I could worry any more about my

gum-chewing habits, a blond-haired girl stepped closer to me. Her skin and hair were so pale they were almost white. She looked me over carefully.

"This is Ariel Chambers," Lani said. "She's our author. Aren't you, Ariel?"

The girl smiled a wide, dreamy smile. "I just love stories. I like to read them and write them." Her eyes grew wide. "Especially romantic ones that have boys in them."

Ariel glanced at my guitar case. "Do you play that? Can we hear it? Wait until I tell the girls in cabin seven that we have someone who can play the guitar!"

Ariel took a step forward as if she were going to rush right off to spread the news, but Lani held her back and sighed. I had a hunch that Lani thought Ariel talked too much.

"You'll love it here, Becky," Lani continued. "There are so many things to do. There's archery, waterskiing, swimming, horseback riding, volleyball, baseball, tennis, art..." Lani ticked off the activities on her fingers.

"And campfires and nature hikes," Meg added. "Lani is a great hike leader because she knows the names of practically all the birds in the forest."

"And there are parties!" Ariel clapped her hands. "You'll love it! Tell Becky about the theme party on Saturday night."

"Every Saturday, we have a party," Meg explained. "Different cabins are in charge of helping with the party each week. Camp Evergreen is a boys' camp about eight miles away. The boys come by bus for the parties and for some of the campfires."

"And some of them are *soooo* cute!" Ariel said, gushing.

Meg smiled and continued. "This Saturday, we're having Fifties Night. We usually play CDs to dance to and one of the counselors is our disc jockey."

"Once, some of the kids and counselors even put together a live band!" Ariel clapped her hands excitedly. I could already tell that Ariel's favorite part of camp was the parties.

While everyone else was talking, Denni stood off to the side, looking almost bored. But suddenly, she pointed at my guitar and her mouth twisted into an unfriendly smile.

"Maybe Becky wants to play the music for the party," she said. "She must be pretty good or she wouldn't have brought her guitar to show it off."

I blinked in surprise. I hadn't brought the guitar to show off! I just didn't want to quit practicing my lessons for an entire month. And, besides, it was something of mine. I thought having it there would help keep me from getting homesick.

Besides, who was the show-off, anyway? Denni Ferguson was the one who had a rich grandfather! Suddenly, I felt angry.

Before I could say anything, Lani spoke up. "It's up to Becky whether she wants to play or not. But I think we should give her some time to feel at home first. Put your thinking caps on. It's cabin eight's turn to help out with the party this week."

Just then a voice came from inside the cabin. "Be sure to wipe your feet when you come in!"

I stared first at Meg and then Denni.

"Katie? Is that you?" Lani asked.

Denni reached for the door and the rest of us followed. Inside the cabin stood a tiny, red-headed girl with a pixie-like face. She was pushing a mop across the floor with so much effort that her cheeks were turning the color of her flyaway hair.

"There's this...gunk...on the floor," she muttered, pushing even harder with the mop. "It's gross, so be sure you don't step in it or bring in more..."

I took a step sideways.

Katie looked up at me with a horrified glance. "Look out!"

I jumped. When I landed, I felt something

rubbery and squishy beneath one foot. Swallowing heavily, I carefully looked down to see what I was standing in.

"Gross!" I yelled, jumping away from the horrible puddle of muck on the floor. "I think someone threw up," I stammered. "And they threw up a lot."

Katie's laughter echoed around the cabin. After a moment, the others began to join in. Everyone in the cabin was laughing except me. I was still staring in horror at the stuff on the floor.

Katie dropped the mop she was holding with a clatter and moved toward me. When she reached me, she bent over and picked up the gross puddle.

"Look, rubber vomit. Isn't it great?" she asked, giggling. "Don't you love it?"

I felt my mouth drop open. I bet I looked like one of the fish in my fish tank as I stared at Katie and her puddle of rubber vomit. But then I looked at Katie's face and I couldn't help it. I had to smile, too. She looked so happy that I'd fallen for her joke.

Her green eyes twinkled happily. "This is the best joke I've played in ages!" Katie announced. Then she threw her free arm around my shoulders and gave me a big squeeze. "I'm so glad you're in our cabin! I've been wanting to use this for a long time. Denni is no fun to play tricks on. She's too grumpy! And Ariel doesn't get my jokes half the time."

Katie giggled again and I noticed that she had a mouthful of braces. "I thought you guys would never come inside! It seemed like I'd been pushing on that mop for hours!"

Lani moved toward Katie. She shook her head and groaned, but you could see by her smile she wasn't really upset.

"What am I going to do with you, Katie O'Reilly?" she asked. Will we ever get you to stop playing jokes?"

"Nope," Katie said. "Too bad I didn't bring all of my jokes from home. My uncle gave me some exploding cigars, but I didn't think I could get anyone here to smoke them."

How was I ever going to make any kind of an impression here? There was too much competition with Katie the Clown, Denni the Ring Leader, Ariel the Airhead, and Meg the Beautiful One.

How was I ever going to stand out in this group? It wouldn't be easy, but Camp Pine-tree was my big chance. I was too close to popularity to blow it all now. I just needed a little time to work on it! And then I'd show them all.

Three

"WHY don't you girls show Becky around the cabin?" Lani suggested. "I've got a few other campers to welcome." She gave me a big smile and patted me on the shoulder. "We're glad you're here, Becky. You'll love it at Camp Pinetree. Just wait and see."

I wanted to believe her.

Denni walked to my side. "This is your bunk," she said, pointing to the top of a bunk bed that was shoved against one wall. "Last ones here get the top beds."

I scooted my suitcase and guitar along the floor to the foot of the bunk beds and looked around. The cabin was very cozy. The walls and floor were rough wood, but there were rag rugs beside the beds. There were rolled-up shades over every window. I figured we would drop those at night and on rainy days.

Someone had brought a reading lamp and a fluffy blanket. I guessed it was probably Ariel.

"Here's your storage area." Denni kicked at a big metal trunk on the floor. "You have to keep all your stuff in there so the cabin doesn't get messy."

"Or mice don't chew things up and ruin them," Meg added, watching my expression.

"Or rain doesn't seep in and leak all over your stuff," Ariel said. I looked at the three of them. I wished Katie would say something. Then I would know they were joking.

I'd just bent to open my suitcase when the door flew open with a bang. A beautiful girl stood in the doorway, her hands on her hips and a frown on her face. Even with her grumpy expression, she looked like she had just stepped off the pages of a teen magazine.

"Hi, Suzanne," Katie said. "It looks like

something's bothering you."

Suzanne's gaze landed on me. "Who's this?" she demanded. I felt like a bug under a microscope as she studied me. And I saw her exchange looks with Denni.

"This is Becky Blair," Meg offered. "She's our new cabin mate. A first-timer." Meg turned to me. "Becky, this is Suzanne Crenshaw."

Suzanne Crenshaw was probably the most beautiful girl I'd ever seen. Her hair was long, thick, and the color of honey. Her eyes matched the color of the stones in my mother's favorite turquoise necklace and her lips were so perfect they looked as though someone had painted them on.

Quickly, Suzanne lost interest in me. "Do you know what Lani just told me?" she asked.

"No," Meg answered patiently. I liked Meg. She tried very hard to be nice.

"She said that I'm supposed to help you guys with the fifties theme party on Saturday night!" Suzanne stomped across the floor and flung herself onto a bed.

"Suzanne hasn't been in a very good mood since she got here," Meg whispered to me. "See, last year, she was in cabin eight, too, and she's good friends with Denni. And both of them just figured they'd be in the same cabin again. Suzanne's been fuming ever since she got here."

I could see that. Her lips were turned into a pout.

Meg leaned closer. "Suzanne likes to be in charge. Her dad owns some big business and she likes to act just like he does—really pushy." Meg's eyes twinkled. "Katie and Ariel drive Suzanne crazy. Suzanne hates it when Katie plays a trick on her. And Ariel is such a chatterbox that she runs around telling everyone what's happened. Suzanne doesn't like to be embarrassed."

"Who does?" I asked.

Meg looked at me for a long moment. "But you were a good sport about Katie's trick." Meg and I smiled at each other and I felt warm inside. Maybe I'd made my first friend at Camp Pinetree.

On the other side of the cabin, Denni and Suzanne were discussing the fifties theme party.

"I think everyone should wear costumes," Suzanne said.

"Where are they going to get them?" Meg asked.

"That's easy," said Denni. "Have the girls slick back their hair into ponytails and tie them with ribbons and scarves. They can push their socks down around their ankles like bobby socks. Everyone can roll up the legs of their jeans just like they did in the fifties. I've seen it all on TV," Denni shrugged. "No problem."

"Lani said we had to do the posters advertising the party," Meg announced. "I could help with those."

"You *have* to help with those!" Denni said.

"You're the best artist at Camp Pinetree."

Ariel turned to me. "Meg won an award for a painting she did. Neat, huh?"

"Yeah, that's neat." The longer I listened to them talk, the more depressed I got. Suzanne was rich. Meg was talented. Denni's family owned all kinds of stuff.

"How do you know so much about a party like this?" Ariel asked Denni.

"My parents had a fifties party once. It was great. More than a hundred people came. They even had a live band," Denni said casually, as if having a hundred people and a live band in her house was no big deal.

I'd thought I had a boring life before I came to Camp Pinetree—now I was sure of it. Worse yet, I was discovering it was even more boring than I'd ever suspected!

Ignoring the conversation, I knelt on the floor beside my suitcase and unsnapped the locks. When I threw back the lid, there were the posters with Eric Richards and Outta Site staring out at me with wide, unmoving smiles. I sighed, wishing the posters were back on my walls at home and that I was there looking at them.

As I moved my things into the trunk at the foot of the bunk bed, Denni and Suzanne kept talking about the party.

"Do you think the counselors have enough fifties music to play?" Denni asked. "We have to have rock 'n' roll music."

"Lani said it shouldn't be a problem," Suzanne offered. "I brought my cassette player to camp this year. Maybe we could even work up some dance routines to music to liven things up. What do you think?"

Meg bounced up and down on her bed. "Great! Everyone loves bands. We could pretend we're a rock group and lip synch all the music."

"That's not different enough. Everyone expects us to plan something really special," Ariel complained. "After all, most of us are old-timers. We know the ropes around camp. Even first-timers like Becky could plan that kind of party."

Even a bunch of first-timers like me, huh? What a slam! I punched my fist into the wad of clothes in my suitcase and Triple Tropical Bubble Gum popped up all over. More than anything, I wanted to show these girls that I was special, too.

"Too bad you can't have live music," I said slyly. Carefully, I pulled my posters of Eric and Outta Site out of my bag. I took a wad of Triple Tropical out of my mouth, broke it into pieces, and stuck it on the corners of my posters. Then, I hung the posters next to my bed. Triple Tropical is great for hanging things on walls. According to my mom it *never* lets go.

Where would we get *live* music?" Suzanne asked with a sneer. "I suppose we could have the kitchen staff play on their pots and pans with spoons."

"And the counselors could blow their

whistles!" Ariel giggled.

"We could clap our hands and hum," Meg suggested.

Denni chuckled. "Great idea, Becky!"

Smart-alecks! I felt a hot rush of anger and embarrassment run through me. My cheeks turned fire-engine red. I had to say something. I couldn't let them laugh at me like that.

"If I'd known about it earlier, I could have asked Eric Richards and Outta Site to play for us," I said before I could stop myself.

Four

THE cabin suddenly became very, very quiet. Five pairs of eyes zeroed in on me.

Ariel was the first to speak. "You *know* Eric Richards? I mean, like, personally know him?" Her eyes were so large they nearly disappeared under the fringe of her bangs. "I mean, as in really, truly *know* him?"

I was about to say something, but before I could, Meg threw herself backward onto one of the bunk beds and squealed, "He's so cute!"

"He must be the cutest boy in the entire world," Katie added.

"And the best singer," Suzanne added.

What am I doing? I wondered. The closest I'd ever been to Eric Richards was the poster

I'd glued to my wall with Triple Tropical Bubble Gum. Now it was too late to admit that.

Denni put her hands on her hips. "How do you know him?"

"I...um...I..." I had to think fast. Denni had a nasty look in her eyes. "He's my cousin," I blurted.

"Your cousin?" Suzanne repeated. She looked shocked, but couldn't have been any more surprised than I was to hear those words come out of my mouth. Why had I said that? My cousins are six- and seven-year-old monsters from Topeka, Kansas. They certainly weren't Eric Richards.

"But your last name isn't Richards," Denni pointed out.

"Eric's mother is my...aunt," I said, hardly skipping a beat.

But I amazed even myself as I heard the words tumble out. Where was I coming up with these things?

"Do you know him really well?" asked Katie.

40

"Oh, sure," I said, sounding more confident than I felt. "Of course, he doesn't visit very often now that he and Outta Site have become so popular. He has to travel a lot, you know—tours and things."

"Have you ever been with him on tour?" Katie asked, her eyes big as Frisbees.

"Not recently. I...uh...went with him once before he hit the big time."

Now where had *that* come from? I must be reading too many movie magazines.

"Where did you go?" she persisted.

I wished I could sink right through the floor and disappear. Even though I knew what I was doing was wrong, I couldn't seem to stop.

"Chicago, Los Angeles...places like that."

Katie gave a squeal that would have shattered glass. "You are *sooo* lucky!"

Meg, Katie, and Ariel were staring at me with envy and admiration. Even Suzanne looked impressed. Only Denni still seemed doubtful.

I'd wanted to come to Camp Pinetree and be popular. Now I'd found a way to do it. Unfortunately, it was all a lie.

But there wasn't much time to think about it now. Meg leaped to her feet and clapped her hands. "Maybe Eric could come for the party on Saturday night! He and Outta Site could do some great fifties numbers. Can you imagine what the other girls would say if Eric Richards came *here* to sing?"

"Oh, I don't know..." I interrupted. "I don't think that's possible. Eric doesn't do little concerts anymore. Just big ones where they can seat thousands of people at once. So even if he could come, Camp Pinetree would be too small."

"But he might come for other reasons," Suzanne said suddenly. "My sister told me that Eric and Outta Site played at a school for the deaf one time. They played their music real loud and the deaf kids could feel the vibrations in the floor and in their chairs. They danced and everything. If Eric would do something neat like that for someone, he *might* come here."

"Yeah," said Ariel. "All the teen magazines say he's really nice." Ariel's pale eyes were hopeful. "How could he say no, especially since he's your cousin and all?"

Things were getting out of hand. It was one thing for me to say I knew Eric Richards. It was another for me to get him to the camp Saturday night. Or *any* night!

"And anyway, what are you so worried about?" Denni asked me. "I mean, you *said* he visits you sometimes. You're not just saying that, are you?"

She stared at me until I felt the heat from her eyes, which never left my face. I gave her a look back.

"Sure he comes to see me! We even had Christmas together this year," I fibbed. "He gave me one of his records."

"The thing is, Eric is very busy," I hurried

to add. "He's recording, doing concerts, all that stuff."

"But he's your cousin," Ariel persisted. "I'm sure he wouldn't mind coming to see you. Right?"

Suzanne, Denni, Ariel, Katie, and Meg all looked at me. I looked at them, then glanced at the poster on my wall. Eric smiled out at me, his blue eyes looking warm and understanding.

"Yeah," I said in a small voice. "But like I said, he probably doesn't have time for things like camp concerts."

The girls didn't seem to hear my last words. Ariel started dancing around the cabin, clapping her hands and squealing. Everyone was making a lot of noise.

"Eric Richards could be our special event for the party," said Suzanne. "If there's any chance that he'll come, we'll have to make the party more special than just silly old tapes and kids in ponytails and bobby socks."

"Maybe we could get the kitchen to cook up something super to eat," Meg suggested. "What kind of food did they eat in the fifties?" she asked.

Denni snorted. "The same kind of food they eat now!"

"Well, how about pizza, then?" Katie asked. "A fifties dance and a pizza party sound good to me."

"Decorations," Suzanne said suddenly. "We'll have to have decorations."

Everyone started to talk at once.

"We'll need streamers..."

"...and balloons!"

"...and posters!"

Ariel spun around the middle of the floor some more, making up her own kind of dance. "This is great. It will be the best theme party Camp Pinetree has ever had."

Even Denni got caught up in the spirit. "Meg can draw the posters, and Ariel and I will ask about getting the kitchen to make pizza that night."

Denni gave me a long look. "Of course, Becky will be in charge of Eric."

Magically, the party was planned, but the most important and most impossible ingredient was left up to me—getting Eric Richards there.

"I'd better go check at the Pine Cone Store right now about decorations," Suzanne said. She headed for the door.

"Wait a minute," I gasped. I felt like I was drowning in lies. "I'm not *sure* that Eric can come. He might be on tour or busy or...something."

"So what are you trying to say?" Denni asked. She gave me a sharp look.

"I just don't think we should tell everyone at the camp what we've got planned in case it doesn't work out," I said. "Let's keep this our secret. Then, if Eric *can* come, it will be a great surprise for everyone else."

Suzanne chewed thoughtfully on her lip,

then glanced at Denni. "I guess that's true," she said at last. "We'd have the whole camp mad at us if we said that Eric Richards was coming and then he couldn't."

"I don't even want to think about *that*," Meg said, her dark eyes round and solemn.

Ariel gave a little whimper. "Oh, but I was looking forward to spreading the news."

Katie made a face at her. "Come on, Ariel. You can keep this a secret. It's only for a few days."

Ariel's lips turned down in a pout. "I know, I know. It's just that it would be so much more fun to tell now"

"It's a deal, then?" I asked hopefully. "No one mentions Eric Richards?"

"Deal," the girls echoed.

"But you've got to *promise* to try and get him," Ariel said. "Try your hardest, Becky. Please?"

Denni just looked at me.

Later, as I lay in bed listening to the crickets chirp and the wind rustle through the tops of the pine trees, I could hear Ariel's words, "Try your hardest, Becky. Please?"

I flip-flopped from one side of my tiny bunk to the other. I'd really done it now. I'd come to camp planning to be special. Now I *was* special. I was probably the biggest liar that Camp Pinetree had ever seen.

Five

IN spite of the mess I'd made by saying Eric Richards was my cousin, I liked Camp Pinetree.

If I hadn't had this horrible, sick feeling in my stomach every time I thought about the lies I'd told and how they were growing, I could have enjoyed everything that was going on around me.

I stayed up late and wrote Eric Richards a letter, telling him about my problem. I wasn't sure he'd even get it in time for the fifties party Saturday night, but it made me feel better knowing I'd asked him to come to the camp. At least no one could say I lied about trying to get him there.

The morning bell rang at 7:00. Denni's feet were the first to hit the cabin floor. "Everybody up," she yelled, as she pulled on her bathing suit. "The last one in the water is a rotten Polar Bear."

I heard Ariel groan in the bunk beneath me. I dropped my head over the side and asked, "What's this stuff about a polar bear?"

Ariel just groaned again.

Meg stretched and stood. "Camp Pinetree has a Polar Bear Club," she explained. "Campers who want to be in the club take a jog on a one-mile trail beside the lake. When they're done, they have to jump in the water and go for a swim, no matter how cold it is."

"Brrrr," I said, shivering at the thought. "That sounds awful."

"If you do it every day you're at camp, you become an official Camp Pinetree Polar Bear. You get a pin and a T-shirt and they make a big deal over you at Parents' Night."

"Is it worth it?" I asked.

"Definitely. Anybody who is anybody at Camp Pinetree is a Polar Bear. Suzanne became a Polar Bear last year. I think Denni did the year before."

That made me roll to the side of my bunk and swing my legs over the edge. I'd lied about having a famous relative to impress people. Now the least I could do was get out of bed and go for an icy swim. Besides, if Denni and Suzanne could do it, I could, too. I'm not a great swimmer, but I do all right.

We all walked together to the beginning of the trail where Lani was bouncing up and down like a rubber ball. "Here's cabin eight," she announced. "Now that everyone's here, I want to explain Polar Bear rules one more time. You have to jog a mile every day, following the marked path. At the end of the run, take off your sweatsuits and go for a swim in the lake. And none of this touching your toes and screaming, 'It's too cold'. Think Polar Bear. The water is *never* too cold for a Polar Bear."

She held her up hand. "Are you ready? On your mark, get set, go!" Lani dropped her hand and led off at a brisk jog.

I glanced around. Denni, Katie, Meg, and Ariel had all disappeared into the middle of the pack of running girls. Feeling left out, I started to jog beside a tall girl with long, black hair pulled back into a tight ponytail.

"Are you an old-timer, too?" I asked as we chugged along the trail.

"No, I'm new here. My name is Lettie Shaw," the girl said. "How about you?"

"I'm Becky Blair, and I'm new here, too," I said, puffing. I should have been looking at the beautiful scenery around me, but I had to watch my feet so that I didn't slip off the trail and stumble into the big rocks that lay along the side. Besides, my feet were already beginning to feel heavy, as though I'd poured concrete into my tennis shoes.

"Are you from cabin eight?" Lettie asked. I nodded.

"Ooooh," she murmured. "I've heard about them."

I blinked. "You have? What have you heard?"

"Just that they're all old-timers," Lettie said. "And that they're really tight—you know, like super close friends."

"Yeah," I said.

Lettie glanced over at me. "I'm just glad I'm in a different cabin. It's easier if you're with other girls who are new, too. You don't have to worry as much about whether they like you."

"I know what you mean," I said. *Boy, could I tell you a thing or two about that!* I thought to myself. But I didn't say anything. I just kept bumping along the trail, worrying about the lie. I had this feeling that no matter what I did at camp, the lie was going to be a part of it. But what could I do about it now?

I was the last one off the trail and into the lake. All the other girls were splashing around, squealing and yelling about the cold water when I pulled off my sweatshirt and kicked off my tennis shoes. Closing my eyes and holding my breath, I ran straight into the water as fast as I could. But when I was only about three feet in, I tripped on something and went down hard—flat on my stomach with a loud slap. I felt myself going under with a glug, glug, glug as the icy water closed around me. The cold took my breath away and I thought I was done for.

I flapped my arms and struggled for balance. When I finally found my feet and stood up, I realized I was standing in water that was only up to my knees. And I heard every girl in the lake laughing.

"She's pretty clumsy, but she'll make a good Polar Bear," someone said.

"Clumsy or crazy!" said another. "Didn't anyone tell her she didn't have to put her head under the water?"

I straightened up and pulled my wet hair out of my eyes and turned my nose in the air.

"Ahem," I said. "We Polar Bears *like* to put our faces under the water." The girls stared at me for a moment before someone started to chuckle. Pretty soon they were all laughing, clapping, whooping, and dipping their own faces into the water. Just to be sociable, I dropped down beneath the surface of the lake again and came up sputtering and laughing.

Out of the corner of my eye, I noticed that Denni had not joined our game. Her hair was still dry and there was a sour expression on her face. She came walking toward me.

"Very funny, Becky," she said. "You're just full of surprises, aren't you?"

I swallowed and felt a trickle of lake water go down my throat. I sloshed out of the water feeling both angry and sad.

"Trouble with your cabin mate?" Lettie Shaw asked.

"No, I don't think so," I said. Lying was getting easier for me.

"Want to go look at today's activity schedule and see what looks interesting?" Lettie asked. "There are millions of things to do and if you don't know how to do something, there's always a counselor to help out, or someone giving lessons."

Together we walked to the main cabin where the daily schedules were posted. I tried to erase Denni's face from my brain and concentrate on the list.

"Canoeing, tennis, swimming, pottery, music...you mean we can do any of these?" I asked Lettie.

"Sure," said Letti. "I asked my counselor about it this morning," she said. "I'm going to take a tennis lesson this morning. How about you?"

I glanced around just in time to see Denni and Ariel walking in the opposite direction of the tennis courts. Being on the other side of camp suddenly seemed like a very good idea.

"Sure," I said. "Tennis sounds great to me. Let's go."

Six

I managed to avoid the girls from cabin eight until after lunch. Then my luck ran out.

As I walked into the big tent that held all of Camp Pinetree's art classes, I saw Denni and Ariel sitting at a table working with clay.

Several girls had already started making pottery. Ariel's muddy gray pot looked like a tree stump.

"How's the celebrity?" Denni asked as I sat down in the chair next to Ariel's.

"I'm not a celebrity," I said as I dug my fingers into some cool, wet clay.

"Anyone who's related to Eric Richards is a celebrity," Denni said.

I put my clay-covered finger to my mouth

and went, "Shhhhhh," but it was too late. The girls across the table had overheard Denni's remark. The buzzing started right away.

"You know Eric Richards?" one of them gasped.

"Eric and Outta Site?"

"Is she telling the truth?" another girl asked.

"Do you really know him?"

Ariel put her hand in the middle of her tree stump pot and fiddled with the clay. "If you guys can keep a secret, *I'll* tell you what we're talking about."

Every girl at the table turned to stare at us.

"Ariel, be quiet," I said through gritted teeth. "We made a deal, remember?"

But Ariel wasn't paying any attention to me. "We have the greatest news!" she told the girls at the table. Her eyes sparkled and she licked her lower lip. "Becky's cousin is Eric Richards of Eric and Outta Site. And he's probably going to come here for the fifties

59

theme party Saturday!"

A gasp ran around the table. Heads turned in my direction.

"Wow!" one girl said, her mouth dropping open.

"He is *so* cute," said another. "And he's coming *here!*"

"Did you see that latest picture of him in *Teen-age* magazine?" asked the first girl.

While the girls chattered, I was dying inside. Some of the girls moved closer. A tall, skinny redhead said, "Would you like to share my modeling tools?"

"Sure," I said. "Does anyone have an apron I can use?"

"Here. Use mine," a chorus of voices yelled.

Aprons came flying at me from all directions. As I looked around, I noticed that Denni was leaning back in her chair watching me. I wished I was getting all this attention because the girls really liked me—not because they were interested in meeting Eric. I was

special now, but my specialness was because of a lie.

"Tell me what Eric Richards is like, Becky. Please?" Lettie Shaw looked at me with eager eyes.

Word about my being related to Eric Richards was spreading through the camp like wildfire. Girls I'd never even seen before were walking up to me and touching my arm—like that would make them closer to Eric. It made me feel weird inside.

"Uh...he's...Eric, that's all," I stammered.

"Are his eyes really blue? Or does a photographer touch them up for posters?"

"They're blue, all right. They look like..." I tried to think of something really blue. "...blueberries."

"How tall is he?"

"About six foot, one inch," I guessed. "That's when he's barefoot," I added, to make my lie seem even more believable.

"You've seen his *feet* ?"

Lettie gave that squeal that every girl seemed to use when she got information about Eric. I wanted to clamp my hands over my ears.

"When you're together, what do you do?" Lettie asked.

I stared at Lettie for a minute, my mind whirling.

"We play games. Old Maid, Go Fish—things like that."

"Does he ever play his guitar for you?" she asked.

"All the time," I said. Didn't she ever get tired of asking questions?

"Can I meet him?" she asked.

"Yeah, sure. Why not?"

As I said it, I wondered how I was going to make Eric appear. It would be a lot easier to make myself *disappear* !

* * * * *

"Are you ready for the campfire, Becky?"

Meg asked. It was almost sundown and we were sitting on the front steps to our cabin, watching a little red squirrel carry away sunflower seeds we'd been feeding him. "It starts in 15 minutes at the clearing by the lake."

"Sure. I've never been to a campfire before."

"Oh, you'll love it," Meg said with a smile. "Let's walk over there together."

I followed Meg down one of the trails that criss-crossed Camp Pinetree. The lake was so still and shiny that it reminded me of the mirror on my mom's dresser.

All the girls at Camp Pinetree went to the campfires, and most were trickling in at the same time Meg and I did. The counselors sat along one edge of the fire, singing and clapping their hands. As the girls arrived, they found spots on the ground and joined the singing.

Katie, who'd been on a canoeing trip all afternoon, came to sit beside me. She scrunched down, crossed her bony knees, and rested her elbows on them for a moment. Then she slipped her hand into the pocket of her shorts and secretively pulled something out.

"See this?" she asked and opened her hand. She was holding a big, black spider with fat, hairy legs.

I jumped backward, and Katie giggled.

"Don't be afraid," she whispered. She glanced around. "It's only rubber, just like the vomit. Isn't it great? I've been thinking I should liven up these campfires a little. Who do you think would yell the loudest if she found this on her leg?"

"I don't know if that's such a good idea, Katie," I began, but she wasn't listening to me. She was already sneaking off to find some poor girl who would have nightmares about spiders all night.

I grinned. Camp was fun. More fun than I thought it would be. In fact, it would have been perfect if I had never mentioned Eric Richards.

Seven

I woke up early the next morning with the sun shining in my eyes. I stretched and wiggled and tried to crawl deeper under my covers, but I couldn't get away from the sunbeams.

"Get up, sleepyhead," Meg said a moment later, pulling at my blanket. "It's too nice to stay in bed. Let's go for our run."

"I just fell asleep," I complained sleepily. "That was hours ago. You have to get up if you want to do your Polar Bear run this morning," said Meg. "We should go a little early, because after that it's cabin eight's turn to serve breakfast in the food hall. We can't be late."

I swung my legs over the edge of the bunk and jumped to the floor. "Give me one minute," I said, as I wiggled out of my pajamas and into my bathing suit. I ran a brush through my tangled hair and popped a stick of Triple Tropical into my mouth. "Let's go."

Since it was still early, Meg and I had the Polar Bear trail to ourselves. Meg looked around her as she ran, admiring the trees and thinking about coming back later to draw some pictures.

When we reached the lake, I kicked off my shoes and pulled my sweatshirt over my head. "Last one in is a rotten Polar Bear!"

I took a clumsy leap into the chilly water. It didn't seem quite as bad as the day before.

In a few minutes, a few more girls showed up and leaped in, too. I didn't see anyone else from cabin eight yet, and that was just fine for now.

There was a lot of splashing around and a lot of jokes, and just about everyone got brave enough to dip all the way down into the water. But the best part was that no one even asked me about Eric Richards! Maybe they'd all forget about him—and my lie. All I knew was I felt like an ordinary person again and it felt great.

*   *   *   *   *

By the time we reached the food hall, Ariel, Denni, and Katie were already there, tying on big red, green, and yellow aprons with "Camp Pinetree" printed on the front.

"You'll have to do your Polar Bear jog after breakfast," Meg pointed out. "Becky and I are already done."

Denni gave me a sour look. But before she could say anything, Lani burst through the door, cheerful as ever.

"Good morning, cabin eight. Are you ready to start serving? Becky, why don't you take charge of the pancakes? Denni and Ariel can pour juice. Katie, you take the sausage and the syrup."

As Lani gave us directions, we all lined up. When the first platters of food were filled and placed on trays, we began to serve. Everything smelled great.

The food hall was filled with long, rough wooden tables and hard, uncomfortable benches. We carried our trays to the head of each table, passed platters around, and then went back to the kitchen for refills.

"Good morning, Becky," said a girl I didn't recognize.

"Hi, Becky. How are you?" asked another.

"Have you already had your swim?" asked a third.

I was amazed by their friendliness. Then, as I passed pancakes from one table to another and watched all the smiling faces, I knew why. They'd all heard I was Eric Richards's cousin. The girls were friendly because they wanted to meet someone who knew Eric. I felt

my shoulders sag a little. My connection with Eric was probably the only reason the girls at the lake had been nice to me, too.

Denni was the only girl who wasn't friendly. She scowled as we served food, and made sure our shoulders didn't touch when we were getting the platters refilled. I ignored her right back, but I didn't feel good about it.

In the kitchen, Katie was up to her usual tricks. "Watch this," she said. She giggled and dug in the pocket of her shorts, then pulled out a gummy, red-and-green candy shaped like a worm. It was gross.

"Watch," she said again.

I had the feeling I knew what was coming next.

Katie dangled the yucky creature over the pitchers of syrup on a tray. "Let's see who likes a little surprise with their pancakes," she said.

She dropped the wiggly, jelly-like worm into some syrup and winked. Without a backward glance, she carried the syrup pitchers into the dining room and began to hand them out. She was already on the other side of the room when the syrup-covered gummy worm came slithering out of a pitcher and onto one of the camper's pancakes. The poor girl screamed until I thought the roof was going to come right off the food hall. All the counselors, including Lani, rushed to see what was going on.

"Don't you love it?" Katie giggled. She looked at me and her eyes twinkled. "I think that was better than the rubber vomit. Don't you, Becky?"

Before I could answer her, she was off and running. The girl who had been surprised with the fake worm was after Katie in a rush. They clattered out the door, whooping and yelling. The rest of the campers in the food hall had stopped eating to join in the fun.

It seemed so easy for Katie to be liked, I thought. *She's great just the way she is.*

I crammed a piece of Triple Tropical Bubble

Gum in my mouth and charged after her. I didn't think the other girl was *really* angry, but just in case she was, Katie might need me. If nothing else, maybe I could pass out bubble gum as sort of a peace offering. It had to be good for something—no matter what my mom thought!

Eight

THE excitement in the food hall settled down just in time for everyone else in cabin eight to do the Polar Bear run. Afterward, we took a nature walk through the woods around the camp. Lani was the leader, and we each carried a book listing the types of plants and animals we might see and a pair of binoculars.

I was straightening the strap on my binoculars when three girls I didn't know walked up to me.

"Hi, I'm Janet," the tallest of the three said. "These are my friends, Chrissie and Mary. Are you Becky Blair?"

"Uh-huh," I said.

"We've been hearing that Eric Richards and Outta Site might be coming here. Is it true?"

My smile faded in an instant. Couldn't Ariel keep her mouth shut at all? Everywhere I went I was hearing something about Eric. Worse, out of the corner of my eye I could see Denni watching us.

"Well, I'm not sure yet, but I think Eric is busy this month," I said.

"Oh," the girl said, sounding disappointed. "Too bad."

"Yeah," I agreed. "We used to be really close, but since he got famous, I don't see much of him. I really hate to ask him to do me any favors."

When they'd wandered away, Denni muttered, "Sounds like you're changing your mind. You don't sound so eager to get Eric here now."

I glared at Denni, but once the nature hike started, I was too busy watching for finches, woodpeckers, and blue jays to think about anything else. We walked for more than two miles and I was sorry when the hike ended.

"Tomorrow, you and the rest of the girls in cabins seven and eight should get your fill of walking," said Lani. "We'll hike up the hills to Seven Falls."

Lani pointed to some distant hills. "There's a beautiful little spot where several creeks come together and make a series of waterfalls. It's very pretty. I try to take every cabin up there some time during the month."

"Is it steep?" I wondered out loud. I liked walking on flat ground, but I wasn't too crazy about climbing mountains.

Lani smiled. "Not too bad, but the woods are very thick. You girls will have to stay together. It's easy to get lost on the way to Seven Falls."

Lani was about to walk away when I grabbed her arm.

"Uh...could I use the telephone at the office?" I asked.

Lani tilted her head at me. "Is everything okay, Becky? Is there some special reason you want to call home?"

I shook my head. "Everything is great. I just need to...check in about something."

"Okay. There's a pay phone in the lobby. Help yourself."

I hurried to the Pine Cone Store and changed all the money I'd carried in my pocket into quarters. Then, I went to the telephone.

My cheeks felt hot and my throat was dry as I pulled from my pocket the address I'd copied from the latest Outta Site tape. My finger was shaking as I dialed information.

My whole *body* was shaking by the time I got the right number and a woman's voice answered the telephone. "Moonstruck Records. May I help you?"

"I-I'd...like to speak to Eric Richards, please," I said. I was so nervous my words stuck in my throat.

The lady was silent for a moment. "Eric

Richards is only here when he records his music," she explained, "but I *do* have a number you could call for more information."

I couldn't believe my good luck! I scribbled down the number, thanked the woman, and hung up.

My palms were still sweating when I dialed again. Another lady answered. "Outta Site is out of sight. This is the Eric Richards Fan Club headquarters. May I help you?"

I cleared my throat and said, "I was just wondering if you knew where Eric was going to be this weekend."

I felt so silly, but I knew I had to ask. I'd been the one who started the lie. Somehow I had to stop it.

"Eric and the band are playing in California this week," the voice said.

California! That was like being almost half a country away from Camp Pinetree!

"Oh," I said. I couldn't keep from sounding disappointed.

"Is something wrong?" the lady asked.

Because she sounded so nice and because I felt so awful, I blurted out the whole story. I told her about how I loved the band and how I'd said Eric was my cousin and half-promised I'd get him to come to Camp Pinetree. When I was done, there were tears on my cheeks. Thankfully, she didn't laugh.

"How many girls go to Camp Pinetree?" the lady asked.

"Lots," I said. "Over 60."

"And what is the address and phone number of the camp?"

The lady waited patiently while I fumbled for the information. I didn't know why she wanted it, but she'd been nice enough to me. When I hung up, my palms were still sweating, but I felt a little better. At least I'd told someone the truth!

At least I'd tried, I told myself. I'd spent all my quarters trying to invite Eric to sing at Camp Pinetree.

Just as I hung up, a big, yellow bus with "Camp Evergreen" printed on the sides came rolling into camp. As I watched, dozens of boys poured out of the bus. Some were carrying baseballs and bats. Others had tennis rackets.

"They're here!" Suzanne screeched as she sprinted by me, her long, blond hair flying behind her. "The boys are here!"

I grabbed Ariel as she ran by. "What's going on?" I asked.

"The boys from Camp Evergreen are here for recreation day," said Ariel. Her pale eyes sparkled.

"Try and get on the softball team. That's where most of the boys will be. If you see a really cute one, ask him to play tennis. That way you'll have more time to talk to him." Ariel squirmed out of my grasp. "I've got to go. I want to see if Jimmy Henders is here. He's the cutest guy at Camp Evergreen."

Ariel vanished down the path. I followed

her, wondering what I should do now. I'm shy around most boys to begin with. It's hard to know what to say sometimes.

By the time I got to the bus, the softball teams had already been picked and most of the tall, athletic-looking boys seemed to be walking away. A few boys who looked like they weren't sure what they should be doing hung around by the bus.

Suddenly, from behind the bus, a tall, good-looking guy with dark hair and green eyes strolled up. He looked a little like the drummer in Outta Site. I could feel my throat go dry.

"Hi," he said, looking straight at me. "Are you playing softball?"

"I got here too late," I admitted, wishing I could think of something funny to say. I pushed at my hair, not knowing what else to do.

"Want to bat around a few tennis balls?" he asked.

"Sure, I guess so," I said. Suddenly, tennis was my all-time favorite sport.

As we walked to the courts, I found out that his name was Ryan Jones, that he was an old-timer at Camp Evergreen, and that he was the nicest boy I'd ever met. What made it even better was that as we walked, I saw Denni staring at me. I'd swear she was jealous.

I smiled and waved at her, as if walking beside a great-looking guy was something I did all the time.

We played tennis for nearly two hours. Ryan taught me how to serve so that my ball went over the net instead of getting caught in it. He didn't laugh when I missed the ball, and he smiled at me for no reason at all.

I was having more fun than I'd ever had with a boy. And it was getting easier and easier to talk to him.

Too soon, Lani blew her whistle and called, "Hey, everybody. Time for some cold drinks and refreshments."

Ryan and I headed over. "The guys from Camp Evergreen are coming back on Saturday," Ryan said, "for the dance."

My stomach did a flip-flop.

"Uh, I was just wondering if..." he paused and I held my breath, "...if maybe you'd dance with me then."

"Sure." I tried to sound cool, even though I felt like doing cartwheels.

"Here she is!" Lettie squealed as Ryan and I came to the clearing where Lani and Katie were handing out drinks. "This is Eric Richards's cousin! She's the reason he's coming to the party!"

It was getting worse by the minute. Now the boys would be expecting Eric, too. I was so frustrated about the whole mess I was about to tell them all that I'd made up the whole story. But just then, Katie moved beside me. She was carrying a tray of drinks.

"Look in the third cup," she whispered.

I looked down into a white paper cup filled

with ice cubes and orange soda. Ryan peered in, too.

"See it?" she asked.

"See what?"

"The fly in the fake ice cube. Who should I give it to?"

"Katie, you're not—"

"Sure I am. I spent a dollar forty-nine for that thing. I'm going to use it."

I'd seen that trick in a novelty shop. It was a real fly—dead, of course—surrounded by see-through plastic in the shape of an ice cube. Whoever got that cup was going to have a big surprise at the bottom of the drink.

Katie drifted away to a group of giggling girls and handed out the drinks. Ryan and I exchanged glances and waited for the screaming to start.

It only took a minute.

Unfortunately for Katie, the girl who got the fly in her ice cube was terrified of bugs and Katie got sent to the administration office.

Luckily for me, her trick kept everyone buzzing and no one mentioned Eric Richards again.

*　*　*　*　*

The next morning I was walking from the food hall to cabin eight when I saw the sign.

My breakfast nearly came up as I stared at the huge, colorful banner strung overhead between two pine trees.

ERIC RICHARDS: WELCOME TO CAMP PINETREE!!!

"Who put that there?" I gasped to Lettie, who had been sitting with me at breakfast. Eric's name was painted in neon colors and underlined six times.

"Cabins five and six. Isn't it great?" Lettie looked proud. "I wanted to tell you, but the rest of the girls wanted it to be a surprise."

It was a surprise all right—just like getting hit in the head with a baseball bat.

"Everyone is so excited. We're just dying, Becky! And it's all because of you," Lettie gushed. "If Eric wasn't your cousin, none of this would have happened." She gave me a big smile. "I'm so glad I'm your friend!"

You won't be glad for long, I thought. Wait until Saturday night comes and there's no Eric. The girls in cabin eight would probably make me sleep outside with the squirrels.

And I would deserve it.

Nine

"WHAT time do we leave for Seven Falls?" Ariel asked as she pulled on her tennis shoes. "I wish I could stay here."

"We leave at noon," Denni said. "Lani said everyone has to go."

"I didn't like it last year," Ariel whined. "It was too far to walk."

It wasn't long before I understood why Ariel had complained. For the first half hour of the hike, I watched birds and picked up interesting-looking stones and put them in my pockets. When my pockets got full, I put the stones in my backpack. But before long, instead of looking at the beautiful trees and sky, I started looking at my sore feet and feeling a dull pinch in my shoulders from the backpack.

To make things worse, Denni was in a terrible mood and she'd decided to take it out on me.

"We're getting behind, Becky!" she yelled. "Hurry up!"

Once, when I got a rock in my shoe and had to sit down to take it off, she called me "Baby Toes." The rest of the time she ignored me. I liked that best.

"How much longer to the top, Lani?" Katie asked. "I'm getting tired."

"Me, too!" Meg piped up.

"Me, three," said Ariel.

Lani chuckled. "It's right over this next ridge, girls. Keep on trudging."

When we reached the top—finally—I sat down and leaned against a wall of rock.

The water met over a series of huge, flat rocks, creating seven mini-waterfalls. If I hadn't been so tired, I would have enjoyed it more. I was almost too tired to eat lunch.

Our rest ended too quickly. Lani bounced from rock to rock clapping her hands. "Time to go! Time to go! We don't want to be in the hills when it gets dark. Pick up anything you might have put on the ground and carry it down in your backpack."

I groaned and stood up.

Lani had started down the hill with the girls from cabin seven right behind her when Denni muttered, "I'm taking the shortcut."

Meg looked at her with a raised eyebrow. "What shortcut?" she asked.

"Oh, come on," said Denni. "We took it last year. Don't you remember?"

"Sort of," Meg said doubtfully. "Are you sure Lani won't mind?"

"Nah." Denni waved her hand in the air. "Come on. It's no big deal."

Meg started to follow. I looked from the two of them to the rest of the girls from cabin eight, who were scrambling after Lani.

"See you at the bottom!" Denni called out

to me in a sarcastic way. Meg straggled a few feet behind.

A shortcut! It sounded great to me. My legs felt like rubber bands and my backpack was getting heavier by the second. I didn't really want to be around Denni, but maybe it wouldn't be too bad since Meg was taking the shortcut, too. And anything that would get me back to camp faster *had* to be all right. I set off after them as quickly as my tired legs would go.

"Wait up!" I yelled. Denni was already partway down a steep trail. She gave me a look that told me she wished I hadn't tagged along, but I didn't care. All I wanted was to get back to camp the shortest, quickest way.

But we hadn't gotten very far when suddenly Meg announced she was turning back to join Lani and the other campers. "This just doesn't seem right to me," Meg said. "I don't want to get in trouble."

Denni looked disgusted, but all she did was

shrug. I looked at Meg, who already was struggling back the way we'd come. Then I looked at Denni, who was having an easier time of it, half-sliding, half-walking down the hill and back to camp.

I shrugged like Denni had and waved good-bye to Meg. I was bushed and just wanted to get back to camp fast. Besides, Denni already thought she was better than me. If I didn't keep going, she'd probably blab all over camp that I chickened out.

I hollered a good-bye after Meg and scampered after Denni. We hiked together without talking. As we walked, I chewed Triple Tropical Bubble Gum, one stick after another. When one lost its taste, I stuck it to a tree and pulled out another. It seemed to be taking forever to get down the hill and it was getting harder. The ground had gotten rockier. My legs and shoulders were killing me.

"Was the ground this rough on the way up?" I asked as I stumbled over a large rock.

"I don't remember this many stones."

"I said this was a shortcut," Denni said. "I didn't promise it would be *easier.*"

"Well, it doesn't seem easier *or* shorter to me."

"Turn around and go back then," Denni said. I shut my mouth and kept walking.

Finally, after what seemed like forever, I looked at my watch.

"Denni, what time did we start down the hill?" I asked.

"About 3:00. Why?"

"It only took us two hours to get up the hill. We've been walking almost two and a half hours to get down."

Denni skidded to a stop. "What?"

"We've been walking for over two hours. I thought this was supposed to be a *shortcut.*"

Denni's face turned pale. "It is."

"We're lost, aren't we?" I asked in a voice that was tiny and squeaky.

The look in Denni's eyes told me I was right.

Ten

"DON'T be crazy," Denni said in a shaky voice. "We're not lost."

"Oh, yes, we are. I can tell. You have no idea where we are."

Denni looked as though she wanted to slap me. "I do, too. We must have taken a little turn off the shortcut."

"A little turn!" I yelped. "If we'd stayed on the trail, we'd have been back to camp a half an hour ago. We took more than a little turn off the trail, Denni."

I shouldn't have yelled at her, but I couldn't help it. The sun was getting lower and lower in the sky and my legs were getting wobbly. I was scared.

"What are we going to do now, Denni?"

Denni looked back up the hill we had come down. "I'm not sure."

"Do you think we should go back?" I asked.

Denni turned around and looked me in the eye. "Do you remember where we came from?" she asked.

I swallowed quickly. "No."

Denni hung her head and stared at the ground. "Neither do I."

"Well, maybe we should keep walking down," I suggested. "We'd get to the bottom of these hills sooner or later."

"Maybe," Denni said, "but once we're on flat land, we're still not going to know where we are." She chewed on her lower lip. I could tell she was thinking hard. And I could tell she was scared, too.

"When I was little and my mom used to take me to the mall she always told me that if I got lost, I should just stay where I was and she'd come and find me," Denni said.

"We're not in a mall now!" I screamed.

"No, but we *are* lost." Denni looked up the hill where we had been, and then down into the thick, blackness of the trees ahead of us. "I think we should stay here. Meg, Katie, or Ariel will notice that we're missing and they'll come looking for us."

"But they won't know where we are," I said. "We're off the trail." I thought about all the dumb things I'd done since I got to camp. Telling everyone that Eric Richards was my cousin was dumb, but following Denni was even dumber.

She'd acted like she was so smart and knew so much about the camp that I'd just assumed she knew where she was going.

Suddenly, I noticed that Denni's eyes looked full and wet. I couldn't believe it. Was she going to cry?

"Maybe you're right about just staying where we are," I said. I sat on a big fallen tree trunk. Denni sat on the trunk, too, as far from me as she could get. "We could sing or something. Then when they come looking, maybe they'll hear us."

"Sing?" Denni asked. She looked at me as if I were crazy. "You want me to sit here and sing?"

I could feel my face burn with embarrassment. "Well, it's not any dumber than getting lost in the first place."

Denni scowled at me. She didn't look like she was going to cry anymore. "You didn't have to follow me down the hill, you know. You were just lazy. You wanted a shortcut."

"Maybe that's true," I admitted, "but if I hadn't followed you, you'd be here alone. Would you like that better?"

Denni looked around nervously. "I guess not," she said at last. "The sun is going to set soon. I wouldn't want to be in the woods alone at night."

Alone. In the woods. All night. The thought made me shiver. I looked at my watch again.

Had Meg or Ariel noticed we were missing yet?

"Do you have anything left in your backpack?" Denni asked.

"Just a granola bar," I said. "I ate my apple and sandwich at the top of the hill."

Denni dug through her own backpack. "I wish I hadn't pigged out up there." She took out her thermos and turned it over. There wasn't a drop of water left.

"Are you thirsty?" I asked.

Denni nodded. "I should have filled my thermos when we were at Seven Falls."

I picked up my own backpack. "I didn't drink all of my water. You can have some of that."

Denni scowled at me. "I don't want to drink your water."

"Why?" I asked. "What's wrong with it?"

"Nothing is wrong with it," Denni snapped. "It's just that it's yours." She swallowed and I could tell her throat was dry.

I thought about saying something nasty

back, but instead I just shrugged and said, "Do what you want, but it's no big deal. I don't mind sharing." I pulled my thermos out of the backpack and held it out to her. "Go on. Really. Help yourself."

Denni looked at me doubtfully, but then took the thermos. She twisted off the lid and took a long drink. "Thanks," she said gruffly, handing the thermos back to me.

"You're welcome," I answered.

We stared at each other for a few seconds, not knowing what to say next. All we could see of the sun was a dull, orange haze in the western sky. It would be dark soon. I shivered.

"Are you getting cold?" Denni asked.

I nodded. "A little."

"Me, too," she admitted. She rubbed her hands briskly along her arms.

Neither of us said anything, but we sort of edged closer together on the tree trunk. Being closer made me feel warmer.

Denni scuffed her toe in the pine needles

on the floor of the forest. "It's weird out here, huh? Lots of strange noises."

"Yeah," I agreed. "Weird."

Neither of us said anything for a while. I slapped at a mosquito and listened to the sounds around us. I thought I heard an owl— but what if it was a wolf or something? Could there be wolves out here? Goosebumps ran down my arms.

"So, you know, maybe we could talk or something," Denni finally said. "It might make the time go faster."

"We've never talked much," I said. "I'm not sure what to say."

"Just say whatever pops into your head," Denni suggested.

I thought about it for a minute, then took a deep breath and began. "I wish we could be friends, or even just get along."

Denni looked up. I could see she was surprised at what I'd said.

"I know you don't like me and I guess when

I met you, I didn't like you very well, either," I continued. "I thought you thought you were too good for me."

"Huh?" Denni asked, puzzled.

"Well, you know. Your grandfather gave the land to Camp Pinetree. And your parents still have a place on it. It's like the camp is yours or something."

"Oh, that," Denni murmured.

"And sometimes you act that way, too—like you own Camp Pinetree and everything has to be your way, especially in cabin eight," I said. I felt myself getting red in the face. I'd probably said too much.

"I guess I wasn't very nice to you when you came," Denni admitted. "I'd hoped Suzanne would be in cabin eight so us old-timers could be together."

"Sorry," I said.

Denni shrugged. "Well, it's not like it's your fault. But then you went and bragged about Eric Richards."

I swallowed hard. Suddenly my throat was dry.

"That made me really jealous," Denni said. "The only important person that I have in my family is my grandfather." Denni sighed. "Really, it was no big deal for him to give up the land. He never liked the lake very well. He likes cities and traffic. He said the lake was dull. He was glad to get rid of it."

Denni looked at me sharply. "But don't you dare tell anyone else I said that."

I shook my head.

"Denni," I began again.

"What?"

"Uh, thanks for telling me about your grandfather."

"No big deal," she said gruffly, even though I knew it was.

"There's something I'd like to tell you, too." I took a deep breath. Here was my chance to admit what I'd done.

"I...I...I like you lots better now that I

understand you," I said.

What a coward! I was going to tell Denni the truth about Eric!

Suddenly, I heard a deep, low growling.

"What was that?" I asked quickly, my heart speeding up.

Denni clamped her hands over her stomach. She giggled nervously. "I guess I'm getting hungry."

"I thought it was a bear or something! I've never heard a noise like that coming from a stomach," I gasped.

"I know. It's embarrassing," Denni said, her hands still clamped around her middle.

I dug into my pocket and pulled out a piece of Triple Tropical. "Here. Chew on this. Maybe it'll help."

Denni looked at the gum for a moment before popping it into her mouth. "Thanks," she said. Denni chewed for a minute and then mumbled, "You're okay, I guess."

Those were the words I'd longed to hear

Denni say and now they'd come—too late. I'd ruined everything. When word got out that Eric wasn't my cousin, my life at Camp Pinetree would be over!

I had to tell Denni. I had to tell now.

"I'm not okay," I whispered. I tried to look at Denni's face, but it was dark.

"What do you mean?" she asked.

"I-I lied," I said. My voice was so quiet that even *I* could hardly hear it. And now, I didn't *dare* look up or I'd lose my nerve. "I lied about Eric Richards. He's not my cousin."

"What?" demanded Denni. She stood up suddenly. "I can't believe you'd—"

But before either of us could say another word, we heard a crashing sound in the woods behind us. I yelped and jumped to my feet. Denni screamed, and we both turned fearfully toward the trees.

Eleven

I couldn't move. I could hardly breathe. I didn't know if I was still screaming or not.

Suddenly, before I could think about what to do, Lani and another counselor, Tammy Wilson, burst through the trees. *They* were the ones making all the noise, not some huge bear or a pack of wolves.

"Here they are!" Lani gasped. She pointed a flashlight at us. I could tell she was worried because the glow from the flashlight was bouncing all over from her shaking hands. "Are you all right?"

"Yes," we said at the same time. My voice was shaking.

"You two scared me half to death!" said

Lani. "When we got to the camp, Ariel came and told us that you hadn't returned yet." Lani looked at each of us and said, "I can't believe you'd take off like that!"

Denni and I mumbled an apology. I knew we'd hear more about it later.

"How did you find us?" Denni asked.

Lani and Tammy looked at each other. Lani shook her head and grinned. "You left a trail."

"Huh?"

Lani held up a piece of tree bark. On it was a wad of Triple Tropical Bubble Gum.

"Every time we thought we'd lost your trail, we'd find another wad of this gum," she said. "I don't know if we'd have found you at all tonight without it!"

I couldn't help grinning. I just *knew* there was something special about Triple Tropical! Now I could tell my mother that it practically saved my life.

"Come on, girls," Lani said, "We'd better get back to camp. It's dark and it's getting late." She gave us a hard look. "And this time, follow me."

Denni and I didn't argue. We clomped after Lani and Tammy, sticking as close by as we could. I felt so relieved, but I was also worried. Denni hadn't said a word to me since I'd told her the truth about Eric. I had no idea what she was thinking and I didn't have time to explain any more about it.

* * * * *

Back at camp, Ariel had spread the word that we were lost. Every girl at camp was waiting for us in the clearing beneath the banner welcoming Eric Richards. When we walked out of the woods, they all began to cheer.

"You're alive! You're alive!" Ariel screeched.

"We were so worried!" Meg said. "Are you sure you're all right?"

"Just hungry," Denni said. "Is there anything left to eat?" Lani took Denni and I to the food hall. There, at the end of one of the long tables, were two plates, set with forks and spoons and glasses of juice. Left-overs had never tasted so good!

Lani sat across from us, her legs curled beneath her, watching us eat.

Denni looked up at her and grinned. "We aren't going to get lost again, Lani. You don't have to baby-sit us."

Lani gave us a serious look. "You girls know better than taking off on your own the way you did. I know that and I know *you* know that now. You can plan on taking an extra turn at morning kitchen duty all next week to make up for it."

No one said anything.

"On the other hand," Lani continued, "you did the right thing by stopping and waiting for us to find you. I'm proud of you for that."

"It was Denni's idea," I piped up. "She knew what to do." I wished Denni would say something to me, but she didn't. She'd hardly looked at me since we got back.

When the excitement settled down, Ariel, Meg, and Katie escorted Denni and I to cabin eight. It felt wonderful to walk into the familiar room. Ariel's lamp was on, giving the place a cozy glow.

I knew I had something to do. I turned around and began to speak before I lost my courage again.

"I have something to tell all of you." They all turned to look at me. I swallowed the lump in my throat.

"I lied." My voice quivered, and I couldn't look at anybody right away. "Eric Richards isn't my cousin. I'm really sorry."

The girls gave a soft gasp.

"Who is he then?" Katie demanded.

"He's Eric Richards. He's the lead singer for Outta Site."

"So how do you know him?" Ariel asked.

I shook my head. "I've never met him. The closest I've ever been to Eric Richards is that

poster hanging on the wall."

Meg stared at me for a long time. "You're kidding, right?"

I shook my head. "It was all a lie."

The cabin was suddenly very quiet. "When I got to Camp Pinetree and all of you old-timers were in cabin eight, I felt left out."

I looked at Denni. "Your grandfather had owned the land. Ariel seemed to know everyone. Meg was so beautiful and so talented and Katie was so funny. I thought I couldn't keep up. There was nothing special about me."

I shrugged and kept talking. "I play the guitar, but not very well. It didn't seem like much compared to everyone else."

"So you made something up?" asked Meg.

"I know it was wrong," I answered. "But the words came out of my mouth before I even thought about them. As soon as I'd said it, the lie grew bigger and bigger. I didn't know how to stop it. And now everyone thinks Eric's coming here." I took a deep breath. "I'm really sorry. Really, really sorry."

No one said anything. Meg turned away and looked out the window. Katie just stared at me. Even Ariel was quiet. I caught Denni's eye for a minute, but then she looked away. I couldn't tell what she was thinking.

I could feel tears starting to fill my eyes. I choked on my next words. "It's been awful. I even tried calling him, but it didn't help. I couldn't get any closer than his fan club."

Finally, Meg turned around and spoke. "You should have told us sooner."

"Yeah," said Ariel. "I wrote home about this and everything. All my friends at home think Eric's coming here and that I'm going to meet him."

"None of my tricks were *this* bad," said Katie. She shook her head at me. "I just can't believe you did that."

"I thought I could fix things somehow. I just wanted to be popular, like you guys are. I never thought it would get out of hand."

114

My lower lip wobbled. "I know you probably never want to speak to me again, but you're my closest friends at camp. What am I going to do?"

I sat on the bunk with my head dropped between my shoulder blades. I wondered if they would try and get Lani to move me to some other cabin. I wouldn't blame them.

Finally Ariel spoke up. "I still can't get over this. I just can't believe you'd do something like this. I am totally bummed out."

Suddenly, Denni turned toward Ariel. "Oh, so what's the big deal, anyway? It's not like Eric Richards would have come here anyway."

Then Denni looked at me for a second. She turned back to the others. "So Becky did something stupid. She said she's sorry and so it's over. Let's just forget about it. The whole thing is getting boring."

My mouth dropped open. I couldn't believe Denni was sticking up for me.

"You're right, Denni," said Meg. She sat

down next to me and slipped her arm around my shoulders. "You didn't have to lie. We would have liked you anyway."

"Yeah...you're still okay," said Denni in a gruff voice. "And now that we know you're not really related to Eric Richards, you seem more...real. Like anybody else."

"But I'll probably be laughed right out of Camp Pinetree," I said glumly. "Who'll talk to me after they hear what I've done?"

"We'll talk to you, Becky," Katie said softly. "Cabin eight girls will still be your friends."

That made me feel better than anything else anyone could have said. I wiped at my eye with the back of my hand. "Thanks," I said. I couldn't think of anything else to say. "Thanks a lot."

Twelve

BEFORE we left for the campfire that night, I dug through my metal trunk to get a sweatshirt. The other girls headed out, but Denni hung back. As I pulled the shirt over my head, she picked up my guitar.

"Why don't you bring this to the campfire?" she asked.

"I'm not very good at it," I said. "I've only been taking lessons for six months."

"That's okay. Do you know a lot of chords?"

"Some."

Denni carried the guitar as we walked toward the fire. I almost stopped dead in my tracks when I saw what was waiting for us.

"Oh, no! Not tonight!" I groaned as I eyed

the big, yellow school bus parked beside a cluster of pine trees. The last people I wanted to face tonight were the boys from Camp Evergreen.

Denni gave me a sympathetic look.

"There they are!" someone yelled, and all eyes turned to look at Denni and me as we walked toward the campfire.

It was strange to be treated like heroes because we'd gotten lost, but Lani had told the story about finding my Triple Tropical Gum trail on the trees. All the boys were looking at us like we were something special.

One boy was staring especially hard—Ryan.

When we sat down near the fire, Denni handed me the guitar. Lani announced, "Let's sing something Becky can play. How about 'Row, Row, Row Your Boat?'"

Much to my surprise, it was easy to play the chords for the campfire songs. We sang until our voices started to get scratchy and the night air turned too cold.

We began to tell ghost stories. Everything was perfect until one of the boys asked, "When is Eric Richards coming? Can we meet him before the party?"

"I want his autograph!" someone yelled out.

"Me, too!" shouted another boy.

Everyone began to chatter about Eric. I traded looks with my cabin mates.

I cleared my throat softly.

"Quiet! Becky wants to talk!" Lettie said.

I knew she thought I had something important to say about Eric's arrival.

"Uh...I...ah...well, the thing is, Eric can't come."

The groans were so loud I thought they'd wake the squirrels.

"What do you mean, he can't come?" a redheaded boy called out loudly. "He's got to come!"

"Yeah," began another. "I wrote home and told my sister I was going to see Eric. She's going to laugh me off the face of the earth if

I tell her he didn't come!"

Everyone except Ariel, Meg, Katie, and Denni was complaining.

Lani held up her hand. "All right, all right. Quiet! Let Becky explain!"

I stared into the fire. "Eric Richards isn't my cousin. I made the whole thing up. He—"

"What! You have to be kidding!" said one boy sitting on the other side of the campfire.

"You're just a liar," another boy shouted.

"Liar, liar, liar." They made a loud, ugly chorus.

"...I wrote him a letter," I began to say, "but..."

"Liar! Liar! Liar!"

"I knew it was too good to be true!"

"She was just trying to be a big shot."

"Liar! Liar! Pants on fire!"

"See if I let her sit with us at lunch again."

Some of the girls from the other cabins at Camp Pinetree joined in. It was getting loud and nasty. A few of the boys even began making faces at me, and I felt my skin getting red and hot in the darkness. Only Ryan didn't say anything. He sat as still as a statue, with a puzzled look on his face.

I picked up my guitar, hoping I could distract them with another song, but somebody yelled, "No more music unless Eric Richards is playing it!"

That did it. I felt tears scratching at the backs of my eyelids. Two big, fat ones trickled down my face. I tried to explain that I'd even tried to call Eric Richards, but no one cared.

Lani clapped her hands and tried to interest everyone in some more ghost stories, but the mood was gone for the night. Before long, the campers were breaking up and walking away in little groups. A few of them muttered when they walked by. I just knew everyone was talking about me.

Pretty soon, I was the only one left. The campfire was dying down. It glowed warmly, but I felt cold inside.

Then I heard someone clear his throat. It was Ryan, standing a few feet from me. His eyes were large and dark as he stared at me. "I just want you to know that what happened...well, I don't think it's the worst thing in the world."

"You don't?" I asked.

"Naw. I've done stuff like that before. Afterward, I'd want to kick myself. You'll get through it."

"I don't know," I said. "This was pretty bad. Everyone hates me."

"I don't think so. They're just disappointed."

I could hear the Camp Evergreen bus driver honking the horn. Most of the boys were already on the bus.

"I guess I'd better get going," said Ryan. He turned to leave, but stopped suddenly.

"Um, you'll still dance with me on Saturday, won't you?" he asked.

My grin was the size of a half moon. "You bet," I said, even though I'd never danced with a boy before. I looked down at my feet, and then back up at Ryan. "And thanks."

Ryan smiled at me. "Everything will be all right. You'll see," he said.

I watched him walk away and get on the bus. Suddenly, I felt that things *would* be all right. I was sure of it. It would take time— maybe the rest of my time at camp—but I'd do my best to make up for the stupid lie I'd told.

* * * * *

Two days later, we began decorating the food hall for the party. Not everyone was talking to me yet, but the girls from cabin eight were, and the rest were starting to.

I was thinking about all of that and hanging streamers when Lani brought me a big package.

"Becky, this was just delivered to you," she

said, looking curiously at the package. "It says 'Important! Deliver quickly.'"

I stared at the package. Where had it come from? I took it in my hands.

Aren't you going to open it?" Ariel asked. "Aren't you curious?"

"Here, use these scissors," Meg insisted. "Let's see what's inside."

Carefully, I cut through the tape and lifted the top from the box. "Eric Richards and Outta Site!" I gasped.

There, in the box, lay a stack of autographed pictures of Eric and his band. A note clipped to the top photo said, "To Miss Becky Blair, from the Eric Richards Fan Club. Hope there are enough here for everyone at Camp Pinetree. Thank you for your interest."

Denni and I stared at each other and then burst out laughing. We were going to have a special treat for the fifties party after all! An autographed photo of Eric for each girl and boy was almost as good as having him there

in person.

While Meg, Ariel, Katie, Suzanne, and Denni danced around the room whooping and hollering, I sat down on a bench and put my chin into my hands. I felt very, very lucky.

Eric's photos would be at the dance.

I'd made some great new friends.

I'd learned a big lesson about lying, and I knew now that being plain, old, ordinary Becky Blair was just fine. Great, in fact!

I grinned to myself, thinking about something else, too. Triple Tropical Bubble Gum had practically saved my life. I guess that means that just about anything can happen— especially at Camp Pinetree.

About the Author

JUDY BAER began her writing career when, at the age of eight, she started publishing her own family newsletter. "Since I was an only child, I had to generate all the news," Judy confided. She not only wrote the newsletter, she typed, designed, and sold all of the copies for 25 cents each. When she was 14 years old, she sold her first article to *Farm Journal* for 10 dollars.

Since that time, Judy has published more than 21 books. In her spare time, she likes to read mysteries, romance, and nonfiction. She also enjoys renovating the old farmhouse where she lives with her husband and two daughters, Adrienne and Jennifer, in Cando, North Dakota, a community of about 1,500 people.

This is Judy's second book for Willowisp Press. She also wrote *My Mutant Stepbrothers*.